For Ash and Kasi. Keep knocking
over jars—life is more fun that way.
—A. L.

For Tom.
Pretty much always.
—D. P.

SIMON & SCHUSTER BOOKS FOR YOUNG READERS
An imprint of Simon & Schuster Children's Publishing Division
1230 Avenue of the Americas, New York, New York 10020
Text copyright © 2018 by Adam Lehrhaupt
Illustrations copyright © 2018 by Deb Pilutti
SIMON & SCHUSTER BOOKS FOR YOUNG READERS is a trademark of Simon & Schuster, Inc.
For information about special discounts for bulk purchases, please contact Simon & Schuster Special
Sales at 1-866-506-1949 or business@simonandschuster.com.
The Simon & Schuster Speakers Bureau can bring authors to your live event. For more information
or to book an event, contact the Simon & Schuster Speakers Bureau at 1-866-248-3049 or visit our
website at www.simonspeakers.com.
Book design by Chloë Foglia
The text for this book was set in Wilke and hand-lettered.
The illustrations for this book were rendered in gouache and pen and ink.
Manufactured in China
1117 SCP
First Edition
10 9 8 7 6 5 4 3 2 1
Library of Congress Cataloging-in-Publication Data
Names: Lehrhaupt, Adam, author. | Pilutti, Deb, illustrator.
Title: Idea jar / Adam Lehrhaupt ; illustrated by Deb Pilutti.
Description: First edition. | New York : Simon & Schuster Books for Young Readers, [2018] | "A Paula
Wiseman book." | Summary: What happens when the story ideas—from a bored Viking to a space
robot—kept in a teacher's special jar escape and get rowdy?
Identifiers: LCCN 2017014405| ISBN 9781481451666 (hardcover) | ISBN 9781481451673 (eBook)
Subjects: | CYAC: Storytelling—Fiction. | Creative writing—Fiction. | Imagination—Fiction. | BISAC:
JUVENILE FICTION / Humorous Stories. | JUVENILE FICTION / Imagination & Play. | JUVENILE
FICTION / Fantasy & Magic.
Classification: LCC PZ7.L532745 Id 2018 | DDC [E]—dc23
LC record available at https://lccn.loc.gov/2017014405

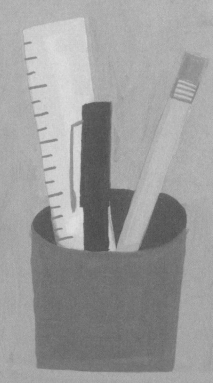

IDEA JAR

Adam Lehrhaupt

Deb Pilutti

A Paula Wiseman Book
Simon & Schuster Books for Young Readers
NEW YORK LONDON TORONTO SYDNEY NEW DELHI

This is my teacher's Idea Jar.

We keep our story ideas in it.

My teacher says a story

can be about anything we want.

A space robot.

A horseless cowgirl.

A giant dragon.

dragon

There's no such thing as a bad story idea.

And there are tons of ways to make a story.

You can write it.

Draw it.

Talk it.

Then, a giant badger knocked on the door.

You can even combine ideas to make your story better.

It's important to create stories for your ideas,

or else your ideas get rowdy.

That can be trouble.

When it's part of a story, an idea is happy.

We need a STORY.
Right NOW!
Let us OUT!
MEOW
PLEASE!
HEY!
It's CROWDED IN HERE.
help!

But when it's not—

Oh no! The ideas!

This isn't good.

Watch out! Those are lasers.

DUCK!

Whoa! Big lizard.

HIDE

Oh no! Stampede!

These ideas need a story.

Will you help?

Let's start with one idea.

Then weave in another.

SPACE ROBOT

Viking

That was great! Now we turn things up a notch.

SPACE ROBOT

dragon

HORSELESS
COWGIRL

dragon

Excellent work! Here's the big finish.

SPACE ROBOT

Viking

WOW! You were awesome.

Look how happy they are.

Now, everyone, back in the jar!

Let's try a story with more ideas next.